A Walk Through the Redwoods

written by **Bridgitte Rodguez**
illustrated by **Natalia Bruno**

For Emma, on every adventure I have with your sisters, you are always with us.

Reycraft Books
145 Huguenot Street
New Rochelle, NY 10801

reycraftbooks.com

Reycraft Books is a trade imprint and trademark of Newmark Learning, LLC.

Text © Bridgitte Rodguez

Library of Congress Control Number: 2023903644

Hardcover ISBN: 978-1-4788-7916-9
Paperback ISBN: 978-1-4788-7917-6

Author photo: Courtesy of Anthony Abuan/Killian Abuan
Illustrator photo: Courtesy of Natalia Bruno

Printed in Dongguan, China. 8557/0523/20217
10 9 8 7 6 5 4 3 2 1

First Edition published by Reycraft Books 2023.

Reycraft Books and Newmark Learning, LLC, support diversity, the First Amendment and celebrate the right to read.

REYCRAFT
B O O K S

The fog hangs thick and low. "It's a perfect day for a walk through the redwoods," my aunt says.

We zip our jackets. "I want to show you a magical place."

The redwoods are among the oldest and tallest living things on earth. Some of them are over 2,000 years old.

We stroll into the forest. The ground
is damp, soft with fallen leaves. Trees
tower over us, their tops disappearing
into the mist.

"The redwoods are witnesses to our
lives," my aunt says. "Like our ancestors
they watch over us and protect us."

More than 200 types of animals make their home in the redwood forests. These include elk, bobcats, raccoons, and even bears!

A chipmunk ***SCRATCH–SCRATCH–SCRATCH!*** at the root of a tree.

A family of deer ***MUNCH–MUNCH–MUNCH!*** nearby.

They see me and stand still. I step closer.

A twig ***SNAP!*** They scamper into the redwood forest.

Drops of water splatter my glasses.

"It's raining!"

I stick my tongue out.

"That's not rain," she says,
"it's the trees."

Redwood trees collect rainwater on their leaves as well
as in their roots. Sometimes when you walk through
the forest you will feel water dropping when it isn't
raining. It is the water falling from the tree branches.

Peeks of sun rays sneak through the clouds. The light catches the striking orange wings of a moving monarch butterfly. "Something so beautiful shouldn't live such a short life," my aunt says.

Monarch butterflies only live for a few weeks or months. During the course of a year, about four generations live and die.

***KE–ER, KE–ER, WEK–WEK–WEK,
CHICK–A–DEE.*** Our ears follow the
sounds. We stop. "What was that?" I ask.

A flash of brown and white flies overhead. I point at
the branches high above. "Birds!"

"Many birds make their homes amongst the trees,"
my aunt says.

The redwood forests are home to more than 60 species, or kinds, of birds—including Marbled Murrelets, species of hummingbirds, woodpeckers, and owls.

We sit for lunch on a fallen tree. My aunt takes off her backpack. We eat salami and cheese on pan sabao, vanilla and chocolate cookies, and apple juice. *MMMMMMMMM!*

"The cookies are brown and white like the birds," I say.

My aunt nods and bites her sandwich.

COOKIES

"Look," says my aunt. "It's a banana slug." I follow her finger. A squishy, yellow slug slowly slithers through the leaves. "Kiss it," she says. "It will bring you good luck."

"Ewww!" I say. "I'm not doing that. We are lucky we found one."

Kissing a banana slug for good luck is lore and not recommended. Their slime includes a toxin meant to numb predators who try to eat them. If you kiss one, you might end up with numb lips!

I take the last bite of my cookie. The wind **HUMMMMMS** through the trees. "Did you hear that?" my aunt asks.

I nod. "The forest is trying to tell us something," I say.

We follow the wind to the edge of the world. The hills and mountains covered with redwoods. "The trees look so tiny from up here," I say.

"Isn't it magnificent," my aunt says. "We are one small part of this great big world."

Streams run through the redwood forests and are home to many animals, including frogs and newts. Fish, such as salmon, steelhead, and trout used to be abundant.

I put my hands into the creek. The water cool and clear. My reflection stares back at me. Next to me, a salamander takes a drink. I move. It plunges beneath the water. *SPLASH!*

Several types of berries grow along waterways in the redwoods, including Blackberries, Salmon Berries, Thimbleberries, and Huckleberries. The California or Pacific Blackberry, *Rubus ursinus*, is native to California. Most of the blackberries found in the redwood forests today, however, are the invasive Himalaya Blackberries.

My hand tangles in a thorny bush. Plump, midnight-black blackberries grow in bunches on a vine. "Can we eat them?" I ask. I pick the berries, plopping them into my mouth. Sweet juice swims on my tongue. "These are the best blackberries," I say.

My aunt smiles. "The redwoods provide the perfect amount of shade and sun for the berries to grow."

The sides of a tree are charred black.

"A fire," my aunt says, "but still, it grows. Persevering against all odds."

I rub the trunk, feeling the smoothness of the black-burned bark. New bark grows reddish-brown and rough. Tiny green leaves poke through, giving the tree new life.

The bark of a redwood tree is a foot thick, absorbs moisture, and is designed to withstand fire. Naturally occurring fires are common in the redwood forests and are necessary to keep the forest ecosystem healthy.

When an old tree dies, new trees can sprout from the burls (large knobby growths) on the stump. These new trees grow around the dead tree, forming a perfect circle, or a fairy ring. As to whether they hold magic powers, that depends on if you believe.

Almost identical redwoods circle us.

"This is it," my aunt says. "The magical place I wanted to show you."

She takes my hand. "This is a fairy ring. Some believe it has magic powers."

We sit inside the fairy ring. We are all here, together. The trees with tops I cannot see. The family of deer creep closer to us. The banana slug slinks from under the leaves. The chipmunk crouches still on a nearby trunk. The salamander swims in a puddle from the recent rain. The birds perch silently in the branches high above."

"There's magic all around if you look for it," my aunt says.

I wrap my arms around her,
"You are right. This *is* a
magical place."

I first discovered the redwoods, *Sequoia sempervirens*, when I went to college at the University of California, Santa Cruz. The campus is nestled among the redwoods in the Santa Cruz Mountains. Redwoods once grew all over North America, but since logging in the mid-nineteenth century, their environment has been reduced to a small area along the coast of northern California and into southern Oregon. Many of the experiences the child has in the story were real experiences I had during my four years in Santa Cruz.

For me, the redwoods are a magical place. I loved hunting for banana slugs, *Ariolimax columbianus*, on long walks to class, especially after the rain. Their bright yellow sometimes easy to miss, even among the browns and greens of the forest floor. Searching for wild blackberries, among hidden streams and relishing in their sweet taste—much better than anything bought at the grocery store. Running into deer during walks to class—and occasionally

wild turkeys, though not native to the redwood forest, roamed the campus grounds. Eagerly awaiting the migration of the Monarch Butterflies, seeing the sky filled with bright orange. Happening upon a fairy ring and standing inside making a wish for a happy future. There is lots to admire about nature, particularly the redwoods. Trees that have existed long before us and that I hope exist long after we are gone.

BRIDGITTE RODGUEZ

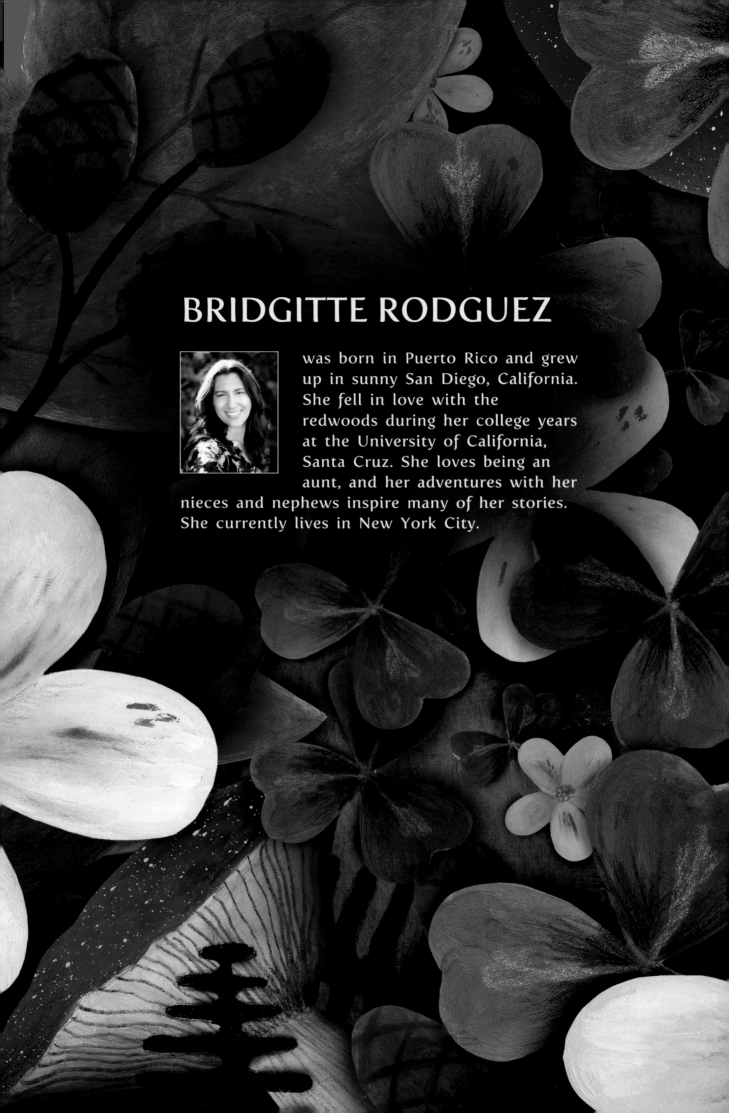

was born in Puerto Rico and grew up in sunny San Diego, California. She fell in love with the redwoods during her college years at the University of California, Santa Cruz. She loves being an aunt, and her adventures with her nieces and nephews inspire many of her stories. She currently lives in New York City.

NATALIA BRUNO

lives with her husband and two cats in a small town called Veronica in the Buenos Aires province of Argentina. She has always loved telling stories and has been drawing since she could hold a pencil. Her journey down the path of visual arts began when she studied photography a couple of years ago. At the same time, she became interested in the world of illustration and picture books, which led her to take several art workshops. Her work tools are traditional: gouache, acrylics, oil pastels, and colored pencils on paper.

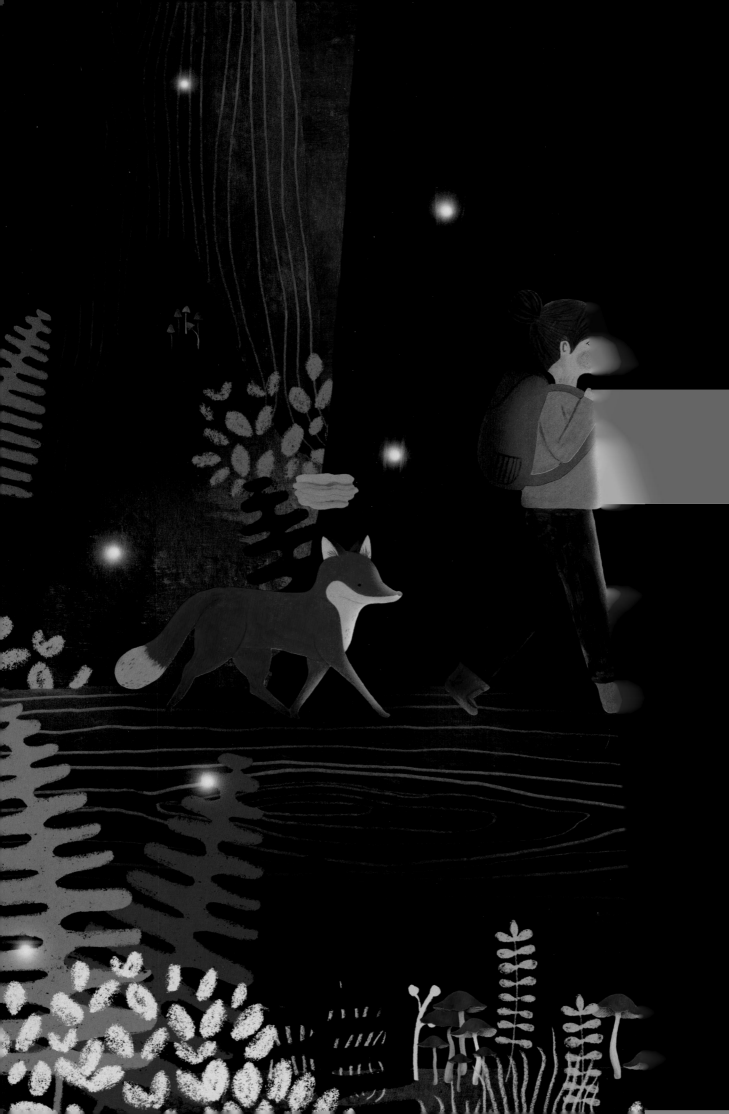